For Toby, Isla and Jesse — A.D.

For my father — V.S.

First published 2013 by Walker Books
Ltd, 87 Vauxhall Walk, London SE11 5HJ
• 10 9 8 7 6 5 4 3 2 1 • Text © 2013 Alexis
Deacon • Illustrations © 2013 Viviane
Schwarz • The right of Alexis Deacon
and Viviane Schwarz to be identified as
author and illustrator respectively of
this work has been asserted by them in
accordance with the Copyright, Designs
and Patents Act 1988 • This book has
been typeset in Franklin Gothic Extra
Condensed • Printed in China • All rights
reserved. No part of this book may be
reproduced, transmitted or stored in an
information retrieval system in any form
or by any means, graphic, electronic or
mechanical, including photocopying,
taping and recording, without prior
written permission from the publisher. •
British Library Cataloguing in Publication
Data: a catalogue record for this book is
available from the British Library • ISBN
978-1-4063-3966-6 • www.walker.co.uk

WALKER BOOKS
AND SUBSIDIARIES
LONDON • BOSTON • SYDNEY • AUCKLAND

CHEESE BELONGS TO YOU!

Alexis Deacon illustrated by **Viviane Schwarz**

THIS IS RAT LAW:

cheese belongs to you.

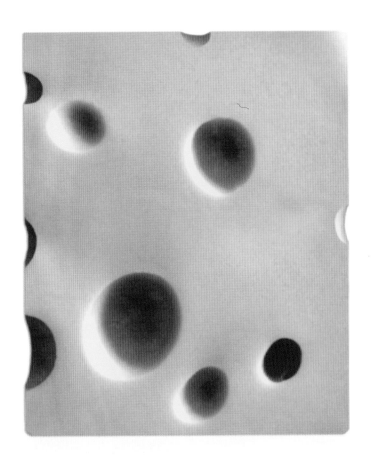

Unless a **big** rat wants it.
Then cheese belongs to them.

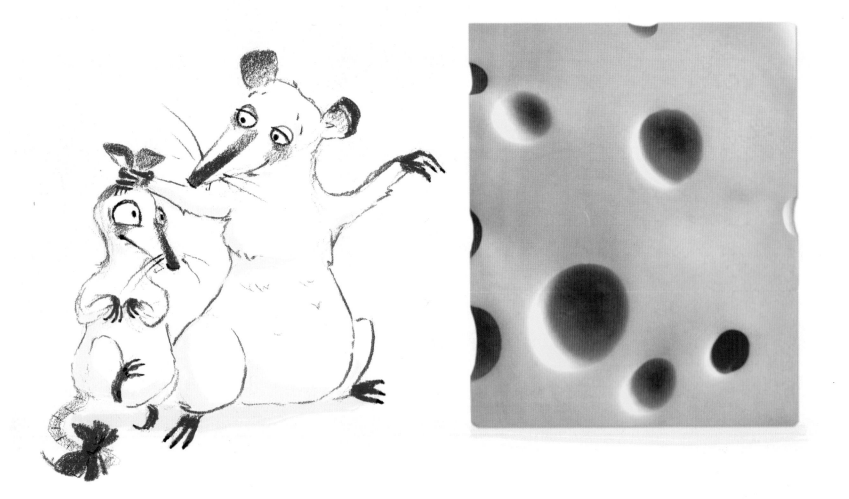

Unless a **bigger** rat wants it.
Then cheese belongs to them.

Unless a **quicker** rat wants it . . .

or a stronger rat wants it . . .

or a **scary** rat ...

or a **hairy** rat ...

or a dirty rat . . .

or a dirty, hairy rat . . . .

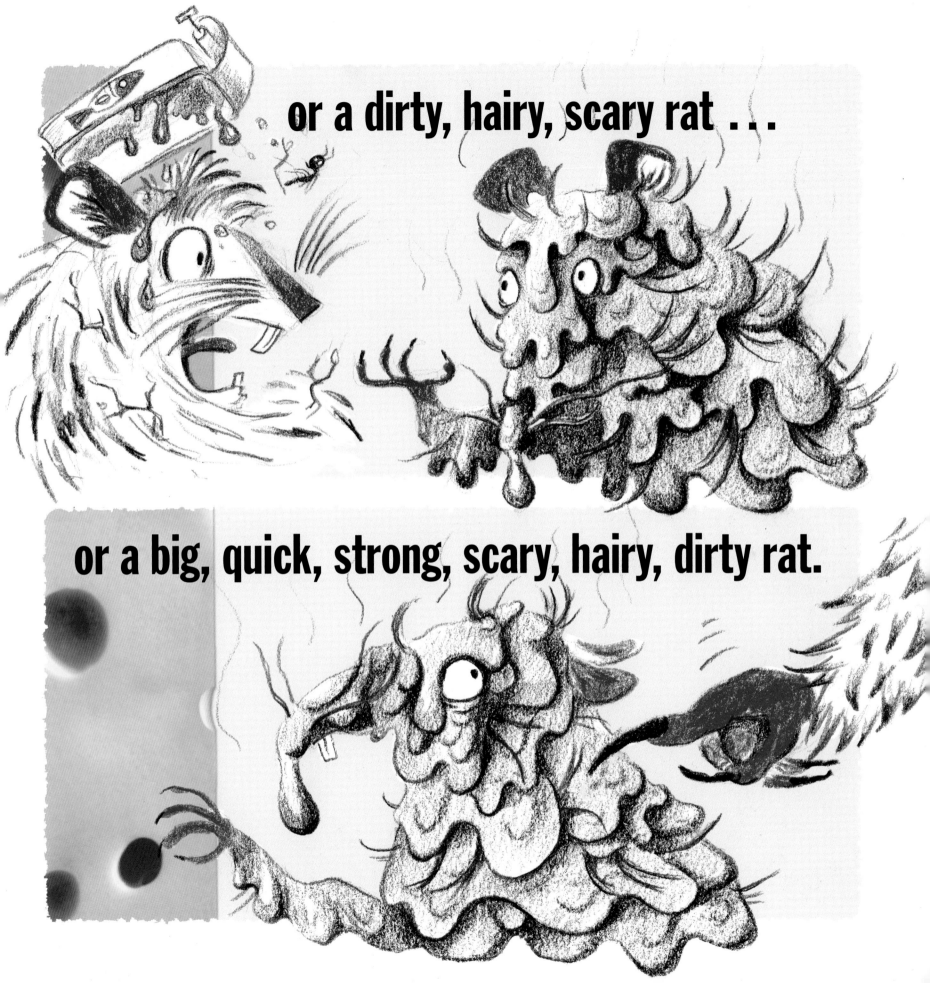

If a big, quick, strong, scary, hairy, dirty rat wants it, then **cheese** belongs to them.

Unless a gang of rats wants it.

Unless a gang of big, quick, strong, scary, hairy, dirty rats wants it.

Unless the biggest gang of the biggest, quickest,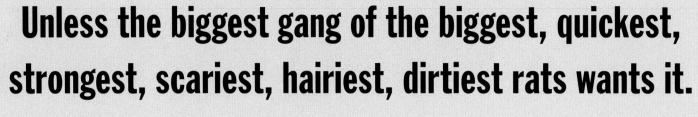
strongest, scariest, hairiest, dirtiest rats wants it.

Unless the boss of the biggest, quickest, strongest, scariest, hairiest, dirtiest rats wants it.

If the boss of the biggest, quickest, strongest, scariest, hairiest, dirtiest rats wants it, then cheese belongs to them.

Unless ...

someone else **wants** to be boss.

Now cheese belongs to you again . . .

if you still want it. THAT IS RAT LAW.

Would anybody else like some, too?